Shine

Bethany Sings Out

D0107008

For all my family – HW

To Felix and Bailey, love from Mom! – MD

~

First American Edition 2020
Kane Miller, A Division of EDC Publishing

Originally published in Great Britain under the title *Bethany's Song*
by Bloomsbury Publishing Plc in 2007. Published in Great Britain in
2019 by STRIPES Publishing, an imprint of the Little Tiger Group.
Text copyright © Holly Webb, 2007, 2019
Illustrations copyright © Monique Dong, 2019
The moral rights of the author and illustrator have been asserted.

For information contact:
Kane Miller, A Division of EDC Publishing
PO Box 470663
Tulsa, OK 74147-0663
www.kanemiller.com
www.edcpub.com
www.usbornebooksandmore.com

Library of Congress Control Number: 2019940421

Printed and bound in the United States of America

1 2 3 4 5 6 7 8 9 10

ISBN: 978-1-68464-036-2

Shine

Bethany Sings Out

Holly Webb

Illustrated by Monique Dong

Kane Miller
A DIVISION OF EDC PUBLISHING

CHAPTER ONE
A Nightmare Journey

Bethany Adams leaned against the bus window and closed her eyes. Just for a minute. She'd had to get up at six and she hadn't had time for breakfast – too much history homework that she should have done the night before.

Her big sister, Serena, had shoved a piece of toast into her hand as she dashed out of the door to catch the bus. Serena loved peanut butter, but she could never remember that it made Bethany feel sick, and so the toast went in the first trash can Bethany saw. She had a horrible feeling that Mr. Townsend was going to say she should have done the same with her history.

It wasn't fair. With her long bus journey to school (and today was a good day – she'd actually managed to get a seat) Bethany never had time to do her homework as well as she would have liked. Mr. Townsend hadn't been exactly happy with the last piece of work she'd handed in either.

She ought to be learning her French for their vocabulary test this morning, but she just couldn't focus right now. She got the book out and propped it open on her bag, as if that would help. But then a warm, dozy feeling came over Bethany and she wrapped her arms around her dance bag and snoozed.

"Excuse me? Hey?"

Oh no! Not another grumpy passenger
complaining because Bethany had her bags
on the seat! She opened her eyes wearily and
prepared to heave her things onto her lap.

"Sorry to wake you – you look as though you
needed that nap. But don't you normally get
off here?" It wasn't someone spitting fire at all.
It was the girl with the purple hair and twenty
or so earrings, who always caught this bus with
Bethany. She was looking worriedly out of the
window. "This is your stop, isn't it?" she asked.

Bethany was sure the girl must have made a mistake – she'd only closed her eyes thirty seconds ago! But she checked out of the window just in case. *Eek!* The girl was right.

The bus was just starting to pull away from the curb. "Stop!" she yelped, grabbing the bell and ringing it about six times. "Thank you!" she gasped to the purple-haired girl, scrambling for her stuff.

Bethany hurtled down the aisle to the doors.

Unfortunately it was the grouchy driver today, and he was making a big fuss about opening them again.

"It's kids like you who make the buses run late," he was muttering. "Wake up, can't you?"

"Sorry." Bethany tried hard to look as though she really was, but it was difficult. This was the guy who insisted on examining her pass each morning as though she were a master criminal, not an eleven-year-old he saw every day. And the bus was always late anyway! At last the doors opened and Bethany jumped out, waving gratefully at the purple-haired girl as the bus drove off.

She dumped her bags on the sidewalk and gave a deep sigh of relief. Thank goodness that girl had woken her up. She'd probably have ended up on the other side of London otherwise.

Sleepily she slung her rucksack onto her shoulder and grabbed her bag of dance clothes. Then she had a horrible thought. Her French textbook!

Please, please, please let me have put it back in my bag, she thought to herself. But even as she scrabbled frantically through her rucksack she knew she hadn't. It was probably down the side of the seat somewhere. Ms. LeBrun was going to *kill* her.

Bethany trudged up the road to school. So far, it was definitely *not* a good day. For once even the sight of the school buildings, with *The Shine School for the Performing Arts* in big gold letters above the main door, failed to cheer her up. She actually felt jealous of Serena, lounging at home watching stuff on her phone until ten minutes before registration at Downsbrook, just five minutes around the corner from their apartment. Bethany was shattered and the day hadn't even started. Was it really worth all this effort just to *get* to school?

Silly question, Bethany told herself firmly. *Of course it is. You're just having a bad day.*

A bad week, something grumbled back. And unfortunately it was true. Bethany felt like she'd been running to catch up with herself ever since she'd discovered on Monday that their science projects were supposed to be finished and hers had been on her bed at home, half done. So she was on the wrong side of Mrs. Taylor, which was impressive as their science teacher was more like a fluffy teddy bear than anything else. And now she was about to turn in some history that she'd spent all of twenty minutes on, and she had to tell their very un-teddy-bear-like French teacher that her textbook was on a bus, probably somewhere near King's Cross by now.

It wasn't going to help that Ms. LeBrun had caught her having a little catnap in French on Friday. Lily and Chloe had done their best to nudge her awake, but they hadn't been in time to save her. And now she hadn't even studied for the test.

Bethany sped up. She needed to get into school and borrow a book off one of the others, fast.

She pounded up the stairs to the Year Seven form room. Shine's school buildings were a couple of old London houses which had been converted and had a whole new front built on – it couldn't be more different from Serena's purpose-built, sensibly laid-out school. It was like an intelligence test for new students just trying to work out how to get to classes. But after nearly half a term, Bethany and her friends couldn't imagine not knowing where everything was – or most places, anyway.

Bethany raced into their classroom and thankfully found Sara with a French book.

"Can I look too?" she gasped. French was first period and they didn't have much time.

"Course," said Sara, sounding surprised. "Where's yours? Left it at home?"

Bethany shook her head. "On the bus. It's been one of those mornings."

Sara nodded sympathetically. She caught the train to school, but her journey was a lot quicker than Bethany's. She'd seen how stressed Bethany got with her nightmare journey.

"Did you fall asleep again?"

Bethany nodded, running a finger down the vocab list to hide her embarrassment.

"I don't know how you manage that trip twice a day, it must be a nightmare." Sara shuddered. "I mean, my train's a real pain, but at least it's quick. I suppose it's all worth it though, isn't it?" she added happily.

It was the same question Bethany had asked herself only a few minutes before, but this time she didn't hesitate. Finding Sara had calmed her down a bit – she was one of Bethany's best friends, after all. Nightmare morning though it had been, this was definitely where she wanted to be. "Of course it is. OK, so sometimes I wish I was like my sister, just popping around the corner to school, but her school is *really* boring. And that's where I would have gone if I hadn't gotten in here."

And if I hadn't won that scholarship, she added to herself silently.

Fees at Shine were hugely expensive because it cost loads to pay all the different dance, drama and singing teachers, as well as the academic staff. There was no way that Bethany's mum, managing on her own since Bethany and

Serena's dad had left, could have paid the fees. It was difficult enough paying for Serena's guitar lessons and Bethany's ballet and tap as it was.

Bethany had always dreamed of going to a school like Shine. She and Serena were both very musical – her sister sang and played guitar in a band at school – and Bethany really wanted to be a singer when she was older. Loads of her favorite stars had been to places like Shine and she knew it would be a fantastic opportunity. But she also knew that there was no way they could afford it. She hadn't even dared to hope for a miracle – she'd just assumed she'd be going to Downsbrook like Serena. At least they had a great music and drama department, and even their own studio theatre. Serena loved it.

Then Miss Collins, the visiting music teacher at Bethany's primary school, who'd been giving her extra singing lessons, suggested Shine to her mum. She didn't want to get Bethany's hopes up, but they did award scholarships for students who really excelled, so…

It took a week for Mrs. Adams to decide whether she should even mention it. After all, what if Bethany got really excited about it and then didn't get in? She would be gutted. Or worse, what if she got a place but not a scholarship? Then she'd know that she was good enough to go and it was all down to money that she couldn't. But Mrs. Adams decided in the end that she just couldn't let Bethany miss out on this chance.

One Saturday afternoon, when Serena was out shopping with her friends, Mrs. Adams went into their room, where Bethany was lying on her bed, reading one of Serena's magazines and listening to music on the phone that had been her birthday and Christmas presents combined. She sat down on the bed next to her and pulled out one of Bethany's earphones. She normally liked the same kind of music as the girls, and she listened along for a bit, nodding to herself.

"Bethany, can we talk for a minute?" she asked eventually, when she felt she couldn't put it off any longer.

"Mm-hm." Bethany turned off the music and looked questioningly at her mother.

"You know we had that parents' evening at school last week?"

"Yeah. You said it was OK! You said Mrs. Thomas was really pleased with me," Bethany said worriedly.

"She was, love, she was. Very pleased. I was talking to that Miss Collins though, about your singing. And she had a-a suggestion."

Bethany just looked at her curiously.

Mrs. Adams twisted her fingers together. "She thinks you should audition for a stage school."

Bethany sat up straighter. "Wow, really? Did she actually think I might get in?" Her eyes sparkled at the thought. "I mean, I know I couldn't go, but it's cool that she thought I was good enough, isn't it, Mum?"

Bethany's mum felt furious. It was so unfair that Bethany should be ten years old and already have given up on her dream just because of money. She was too young to have to think like that. She swallowed. "She thinks there's maybe a chance that you could go," she said cautiously. "Just a chance, mind."

Bethany shook her head. "No way, Mum. Serena and I looked online. Have you seen how much those places cost? It's like thousands each *term*!"

"I know." Bethany's mum didn't mention that she'd spent ages looking at the same websites, sadly scribbling sums on little scraps of paper. Bethany was right. There was no way. Unless…

"Miss Collins reckons you could maybe apply for a scholarship. They have them, apparently, at these places. They'd cover the fees and give you something toward your uniform. We'd just have to find the money to get you there every day. She suggested the Shine School – she said she's got some friends who teach there and it's very good."

Bethany was gazing at her like she'd suggested a trip to Disney World. "That was one of the websites we looked at, Mum! It's one of the best schools in the country. Jasmine Day went there!" She waved her phone at her mum – they'd just been listening to Jasmine's debut album.

"Bethany, listen. It *is* one of the best schools in the country and it's incredibly hard to get into. It's going to be even harder to get a scholarship. And I'm sorry, love, but it's like you say – the fees are huge. Without the scholarship we couldn't do it. So it's probably a thousand to one chance." She shrugged helplessly at her daughter. "Do you want to try?"

Of course Bethany did. She totally understood everything her mum had said about it being really unlikely she'd get in *and* get a scholarship, but she had to at least *try*, didn't she?

And the thousand to one chance had worked. Bethany thought it was probably because she'd been quite relaxed at the audition – it had all seemed so unlikely that she hadn't really gotten too keyed up about it. But now that she was here, it was better than she could ever have imagined, with dance, theatre and music classes every afternoon taught by brilliant teachers. It was just the traveling that was such a nightmare. Still, she had no right to moan. Loads of the students made crazy journeys to get to Shine. She was by no means the only one.

"Of course it's worth it," she told Sara, in a voice that was almost naturally cheerful. "I could do without grumpy bus drivers, that's all. And grumpy French teachers. Ms. LeBrun's going to kill me."

Sara really wanted to say something encouraging, but she had to settle for "Mmmm." Their French teacher was OK, but she wasn't known for her patience. "Perhaps if you do really well on this test you could tell her about your book afterward," she added hopefully.

"Yeah," Bethany agreed. "Course, there's one snag with that."

"Mmm, but you're quite good at French normally. Here, have the book." Sara thrust the book at Bethany. "I reckon I've learned it enough. I wouldn't like to give Ms. LeBrun a heart attack by getting too many right."

"There they are!" Lily and Chloe raced into the classroom, both grinning, and hurtled to a stop by Sara and Bethany.

"We did it!" Chloe squeaked, dancing up and down. "We got the parts in *Little Women*, both of us. Can you believe it?"

"That's brilliant!" Sara gasped. "The parts you wanted?"

Lily nodded. "Yes, I'm going to be Beth and Chloe's got Amy. It's just perfect!"

Bethany hugged them both quickly. "That's so exciting! Well done! Oh wow, it's amazing, I can't believe you're going to be on TV!" She couldn't help feeling a tiny hint of jealousy. She wished *she* had an audition – so far she hadn't even been considered for anything. There was no way she wanted Lily and Chloe to see that though – she really was pleased for them.

Chloe looked like she couldn't stand still for

excitement. "We're going to be staa-aars!" she sang, twirling around, her curly red hair flying around her head.

"You're going to have to calm down sometime, Chloe! I bet you didn't sleep at all!" Sara giggled. "Hey, why didn't you call us?"

Lily and Chloe exchanged embarrassed glances. "We-ell," Lily explained slowly. "I didn't know if Chloe had gotten a part and she didn't know if I had—"

"I did ask Ms. Shaw, but she wouldn't tell me," Chloe put in.

"So we both kind of wanted to wait until we'd found that out before we told you. I mean, I don't think I'd have felt the same way about it if Chloe hadn't gotten a part too."

Chloe nodded. "And it seemed a bit weird to call and ask Lily, so I was waiting until this morning. Then we saw each other in the entrance hall and it was totally obvious!"

"I don't think I've stopped grinning since Ms. Shaw phoned last night," Lily agreed.

"What did your mum say?" Bethany asked gently. Lily had been under real pressure from her mum. She was an actress and she'd been desperate for Lily to act too – whatever it took.

Lily smiled and Bethany thought she hadn't seen her look so relaxed and happy in ages. "That's the best part! I had this really good talk with my mum after the audition.

She's promised to stop trying to run my life for me!"

"So is she going to back off?" Sara asked.

Lily nodded enthusiastically. "She said she'll still help with whatever I want, but I have to ask her. She's keeping well out of it. And you know what, now that she's said that, I think I probably will ask her to help me with learning my scenes – she does have really good ideas."

"Hey, do you think she'd coach me too?" Chloe asked.

Bethany shook her head in amazement. "I totally can't believe you're talking about the same person! After what you said on Monday!"

Seeing Lily and Chloe so excited, Bethany couldn't help feeling that sharp sense of jealousy again.

Why wasn't this happening for her too?

CHAPTER TWO
Bethany's Turn

Chloe and Lily's big news pretty much axed any further French studying, so Bethany wasn't feeling too confident as Ms. LeBrun strode into the classroom half an hour later.

She loved shopping, even though she never had much allowance, so shouldn't that make learning the names of shops easier? But it didn't seem to be working that way. She reckoned she was OK on the list of things you could buy at the *boulangerie*, though. In fact, she could really do with a *pain au chocolat* right now.

Everyone sighed and shoved away their textbooks as their smartly dressed teacher beamed evilly at them. "Are we all ready for our little vocabulary test?" she asked sweetly. She perched herself on the desk in front of them with the book and proceeded to read out a list of words in English for them to turn into French. Bethany could have sworn most of them had not been on the list they'd been told to learn. What on earth was the French for sausages?

She grimly filled in as many as she could,

but she didn't have a good feeling about it, and she cast a panicky glance at Sara. Her friend was scribbling and gazing raptly at her paper, her long blond hair falling in a curtain that hid her face.

Bethany quickly scanned around the rest of their table. Lily was concentrating like Sara, and Chloe – surprise, surprise – was staring into space with a happy smile on her face. As Bethany watched, Chloe suddenly caught herself in her daydream and stared back down at her test paper. French clearly wasn't the first thing on her mind today.

Ms. LeBrun got them to mark each other's tests and Sara's face was not encouraging as she checked Bethany's answers. As she counted them she glanced apologetically at her friend. "Only eight right. I'm sorry, Bethany."

Eek! Eight out of twenty? Ms. LeBrun was going to love that.

"I only got nine," Chloe said encouragingly. "It was a really hard test. Don't worry about it."

Mmmm. That was all very well for Chloe to say, but she wasn't at Shine on a scholarship – one that was "conditional upon performance." Which meant that Bethany had to do really well not only in the drama and dance classes, but academic work too. And after her disastrous performance in science, history and now French this week, no one was going to say she was managing that.

Bethany twisted a wisp of hair around her finger miserably. Just how useless did you have to be to get thrown out of stage school? Or have your scholarship taken away? Because for her, it would be the same thing.

It wasn't even as if she'd been doing so well in her stage classes that they'd overlook the academics, she worried to herself. Sara had her part in *Mary Poppins*, and now

Chloe and Lily had done brilliantly in the auditions for a major drama series. No one had even mentioned Bethany auditioning for anything. If things carried on like this, maybe the school was going to start thinking the scholarship should have gone to somebody else.

Luckily, Bethany wasn't the only one who'd done badly on the test – Chloe's friend Sam came bottom with four out of twenty. But she did get a particularly unimpressed glare from Ms. LeBrun when she told the teacher her score. She supposed she couldn't expect much else after dozing off in the previous lesson. Now was definitely not the time to admit she'd left her French book on the bus. So it was a bit of a disaster when Ms. LeBrun saw her sharing Sara's book and snapped, "Bethan-ee! Your book, where is it?" She always sounded more French when she was cross.

Bethany just stared at her with her mouth

hanging open like a goldfish, wondering what
on earth to say. But Sara gave Ms. LeBrun her
best smile.

"Actually this is Bethany's book, Ms.
LeBrun. I left mine in my locker and
Bethany's sharing with me. Sorry!"

Sara had pulled out all the stops and
gotten seventeen on the vocab test, so she
was in Ms. LeBrun's good books. The French
teacher just smiled and nodded, and carried
on with the lesson.

"Thank you!" Bethany whispered as soon as

Ms. LeBrun wasn't looking.

"No problem." Sara grinned. "I think she might have bitten your head off otherwise!"

Bethany managed to survive the rest of the morning without any more comments on her work. They had science but she'd handed in her project the day before with a groveling note, and Mrs. Taylor seemed to be OK about it.

She was still feeling a bit down at lunchtime, though. She picked at her salad while the others eagerly discussed the *Little Women* auditions.

Sara nudged her. "Hey, are you OK?" she asked quietly, as Chloe and Lily argued about what Ms. Shaw, the school's agent, had said would happen next.

Bethany shrugged. "Just worrying about that book. I can't keep 'lending' it to you!"

Sara grimaced. "Maybe Ms. LeBrun will have calmed down by next lesson," she said hopefully.

"It's *possible*," said Bethany thoughtfully. Then they looked at each other and started giggling. "Calm" and "Ms. LeBrun" just didn't really go together all that well. Still, Bethany felt a bit better.

They had singing that afternoon – her favorite class. Even though Mr. Harvey could be difficult, he was a brilliant teacher and Bethany knew that her voice was improving all the time in his classes.

Today Mr. Harvey seemed to be even more unpredictable than usual. There was a kind of suppressed excitement about him and his warm-up exercises went one step beyond weird. "Chocolate!" he announced dramatically as he sat down at the piano. Everyone looked hopeful. "A brilliant word for working the facial muscles. Chocolate, chocolate, chocolate, chocolate, chocolate!" He sang up the scale to demonstrate, making elaborate chewing motions as he went. "Everybody! Work those mouths!"

Everyone obediently chewed away on their imaginary chocolate – as well as they could while laughing anyway. But he was right, it really did seem to loosen up their mouth muscles, which was good, as Mr. Harvey was always yelling in the middle of songs that no one in the class opened their mouths wide enough.

After nearly an hour of picking a song to pieces, Mr. Harvey crashed down the piano lid. Everyone jumped, but for once this didn't seem to be because he was about to have a rant. He grinned at them all and Bethany guessed that he was finally about to tell them why he was looking like a cat that had gotten a whole carton of cream.

"I have good news for some of you," he purred, standing up and leaning on the piano top. "Who's heard about the Wish concert at the Albert Hall next month?"

"That big charity concert, sir?" someone piped up from the back.

"Exactly. 'Big' being the operative word. Massive charity concert with loads of top stars, all in aid of children's charities. Well, since it's to raise money for children, they'd like some children in it. Which is where you all come in."

"Us?" Bethany squeaked delightedly. "Really? Jasmine Day's singing in that concert and loads of other amazing people!"

"Not all of you. Just ten people from Years Seven and Eight. But you, Bethany, I'm happy to say, are on my little list." Bethany was actually jumping up and down and hugging Lily by now.

"Wow, I'm so jealous," Lily breathed. "Well done, Bethany!"

"Let me see. Year Sevens. Yes. Bethany, Chloe, Sam – was I out of my mind? Sam, you'd better watch yourself—"

"Yes, sir," Sam agreed, with a massive grin on his face. He was one of the class's biggest jokers, but he did have a very good voice.

Mr. Harvey carried on reading out names. "Jade, Daisy and Aiden. And remember you all, any bad reports and you'll be out – this is a very prestigious event for the school to be asked to take part in. Do not let me down!"

He was doing his super-fearsome scowl now, but the six people he'd named were too excited to notice.

"Chloe!" Bethany skittered over to hug her. "This is so cool! We're going to be in the same concert hall with Jasmine Day!"

"Better than that, Bethany." Mr. Harvey went back to the Cheshire cat impression. "Jasmine Day is the singer you'll actually be performing with. You'll be part of her backing group. She requested students from Shine — you know she was a student here herself."

"Did you teach her, Mr. Harvey?" Chloe asked breathlessly. Bethany was speechless by now.

"Uh-huh. Never opened her mouth enough. Very lazy." Mr. Harvey sniffed disgustedly and most of the class fell about giggling, imagining Jasmine Day being yelled at by Mr. Harvey for not opening her mouth!

"Nice voice, though," he admitted grudgingly, which was very high praise from him. "Right, the bell's about to go. I'll let you know about the rehearsal schedule – it's going to be mostly after school."

Chloe was looking worried as they strolled over to the drama studio. "I hope the rehearsals aren't going to clash with any of the *Little Women* stuff. I don't want to miss out on either of them!"

"They probably won't," Lily said reassuringly. "That's only going to be one or two days, for costume fittings and that sort of thing. There's ages till the actual filming."

Finally Bethany could listen to them discussing their parts without feeling a bit like a loser. Now that this brilliant chance had come through for her, she could actually admit that that was how she'd been thinking of herself. "You spoiled brat," she said jokingly to

Chloe, shaking her head and smiling. "If only we all had such problems!"

Chloe elbowed her. "Us geniuses," she said grinning. "Though actually, if it hadn't been for *Mary Poppins*, there's no way he'd have chosen me – it would have been you, Sara, your voice is way better. Don't you mind?"

Sara shook her head. "Oh, maybe a tiny bit, but not really. I'm more into musicals anyway. You know being in *Mary Poppins* is my dream part."

Bethany shook her head. She could see that Sara really meant it, but she couldn't see *how*. A chance to sing with Jasmine Day – even if only for one night – wasn't something she could bear to miss.

She floated through their acting class in a delighted haze, but her commute home had never seemed longer. She was desperate to get back and tell Serena and Mum, who'd be home from her job at the hair salon soon after Bethany got there.

Serena was curled up on the sofa with yet more toast and peanut butter – *ugh!* – and a magazine. She looked up in surprise as Bethany hurtled into the apartment. This whirlwind clearly had news.

Bethany threw herself down on the sofa next to her sister. "I thought so," she said joyfully, grabbing Serena's magazine so she could look at the article Serena was currently dripping peanut butter on.

"Hey!" squawked Serena, nearly losing her toast as she tried to grab the magazine back.

But Bethany wasn't listening. "Look!" She stabbed her finger at the feature. There was a big photo of Jasmine Day, grinning into the camera and wearing a Wish T-shirt. "I thought

I'd read something about it. You see this –
about the big charity concert she's singing in?
I'm singing in it too! Ten of us from school are
going to be her backing group!"

"No way!" said Serena suspiciously. "You *are*
kidding, aren't you?"

"Uh-uh! I'm not, we found out in singing
today." Bethany read the article again eagerly,
hoping to find out some interesting details.
Mr. Harvey had been irritatingly short on
the more gossipy side of things. But it was
mostly about how Jasmine Day had been really
excited to be appearing in the concert because
she'd suffered similar problems to some of the
children Wish was trying to help. "Wow, I
wonder what…" Bethany murmured, pointing
this out to Serena.

Serena was still trying to get her head
around her little sister singing at the Albert
Hall. So far she hadn't really felt jealous of

Bethany going to Shine – she liked her own school and Shine sounded too much like hard work – but singing with Jasmine Day? That was amazing.

"I can't believe it," she said, grabbing the magazine back. "You're really going to be in this? Wait till I tell everyone at school! Isn't it going to be on TV?"

"I think so," Bethany said happily. "I can't wait to tell Mum!"

On cue there was the sound of a key in the front door.

Mrs. Adams was slightly surprised to be met at the door by both her daughters waving a magazine and shrieking. It took a while for her to work out what was going on, but then she decided they had to celebrate with pizza and a film.

It was a bit of a downer for Bethany to have to get up at six again the next morning and scramble through the homework she hadn't managed to fit in the night before – which was most of it, although she hadn't let Mum know that. But as she stood yawning at the bus stop, Bethany just had to think "concert" for it all to be worthwhile. Unfortunately there was nowhere to sit on the bus, so she clung on to the rail and daydreamed.

"Hey!" It was the purple-haired girl from yesterday again. Bethany looked around in a panic. Surely she hadn't missed her stop? She couldn't have gone to sleep standing up, could she?

The older girl laughed. "No, it's OK! You've got ages. You really were away with the fairies. Anyway, I've got something for you." She rummaged around in a cool straw bag covered in flowers. "Got it here somewhere." At last she triumphantly brought out a book. "You left it yesterday when you had to get off in such a hurry."

"My French book!" Bethany felt like hugging her. "Thank you!" It seemed like suddenly everything was going to be all right!

"Not a problem. Do you go to some kind of special school? I can't believe you do this journey every day – it's bad enough me doing it to get to college."

Bethany nodded proudly. "I go to a stage school," she explained. "Shine, in Bloomsbury."

"I can see why you make the effort then!" The older girl smiled at her. "Wow. Would I have seen you in anything?"

Bethany blushed. This felt so cool! "No, not yet. But I'm going to be in a big charity concert soon. The Wish concert at the Albert Hall? We're singing with Jasmine Day."

The girl with purple hair looked very impressed. "How do you fit that kind of thing in with schoolwork though?" she asked interestedly. "I mean, you can't have much time at home as it is."

Bethany stared at her. This wasn't even something she'd considered, although now, after the disasters of yesterday morning, she wondered how she could have been so silly. How on earth was she going to fit in the rehearsals and her homework and the traveling? She never got home much before five thirty now, and Mr. Harvey had said the Wish rehearsals would be after school. Homework wasn't going to get a chance! And there were hardly any buses home later in the evening. Bethany looked stricken and the older girl looked back worriedly.

"Hey, sorry, did I say something wrong? I was just wondering."

"No, no, it's OK," Bethany stammered. "I just hadn't really thought about it much yet. That kind of thing, I mean. We only found out we were in it yesterday."

"I'm sure it'll be OK. Who cares about homework anyway?" The girl grinned at her.

Bethany tried to smile back as though she agreed, but she knew she didn't have a choice. She *had* to care about homework, however much she didn't want to. And she couldn't help worrying about all the trouble she'd had with work lately. It was awful even to think about it – but maybe she couldn't be in the concert after all.

CHAPTER THREE
Leaving Home

Bethany hurried off the bus and headed into school. The worst thing was she couldn't even discuss this with Chloe, Lily and Sara. Or not without hiding what was really bothering her, anyway. She'd decided ages ago that she wasn't going to tell anyone about her scholarship. She just wasn't sure how people would react – and she didn't really like the idea of everyone knowing her mum couldn't afford to pay the school's fees.

She knew that Sara's grandma paid half of hers, but she got the impression that that was more because Sara's parents didn't really want to be shelling out for a school they disapproved of, rather than because they couldn't afford it. Sara's gran had been a professional dancer and she was delighted that her granddaughter had won a place at Shine. And Chloe and Lily's parents obviously had no trouble paying for them. Bethany was pretty sure Shine only gave one scholarship a year, so obviously everyone else in her class had parents who could pay the fees, and Bethany really didn't want to be the odd one out.

What on earth was she going to do? Bethany seriously couldn't imagine going to find Mr. Harvey and telling him she couldn't do the concert after all. She'd probably be able to make him understand eventually, but he'd go ballistic at first. She shuddered. No, she needed to find someone sympathetic to talk to – someone on the staff, who must all already know about her scholarship. She trudged through the hall, looking miserable and wondering who she could ask. She was staring at the floor, so she didn't notice Miss Jasper, their ballet teacher, coming the other way – until she walked into her.

"Oops!" Luckily Miss Jasper was really nice and she put out her hands to catch Bethany's shoulders and steady her. "Watch out, Bethany! Are you OK?" she added, looking at Bethany's eyes, which were red rimmed from trying not to cry. Knowing that she was in the concert with Jasmine Day had been like a dream come true for all of eighteen hours, but ever since the girl on the bus had made her realize that she couldn't be in the concert, Bethany had felt like howling. She didn't want anyone to see her upset though, or to think that she was a baby.

Bethany sniffed. Miss Jasper was being *too* nice and that was fatal. A large tear dripped down the side of her nose, even as she nodded brightly. "I'm fine," she muttered. Then a thought struck her.

Miss Jasper wasn't actually anything to do with the concert, of course, but maybe she could give her some advice, maybe even talk to Mr. Harvey for her. But actually telling someone she was giving up the chance of a lifetime was too much. She just couldn't. Bethany made a strange gulping noise and looked around for somewhere to run.

Miss Jasper was still holding her. She steered Bethany into an empty office off the hallway and directed her toward a chair. "Talk to me," she said firmly. She could see that trying to comfort Bethany was just going to make her worse. "What is it?"

Her brisk voice calmed Bethany down and she managed to hold back her tears. She explained as quickly as she could, feeling really embarrassed as she mentioned the scholarship and her problems with work. Luckily Miss Jasper didn't seem to care very much about that.

"I see," she said thoughtfully. "Mmm. We obviously need to do something, but I don't think giving up the concert is the answer, Bethany. After all, that's what you're here for, isn't it?"

"You don't think so?" Bethany looked up at her in sudden hope. Then she sighed.

"But I just don't see how I can fit the rehearsals in. There isn't anything else I can do."

"Of course there is!" The ballet teacher shook her head, smiling. "Bethany, we have this kind of problem all the time! Loads of the students come from a long distance. A couple of girls in Year Nine even moved down to live with relatives when they got their places. They go home at weekends. And that's the kind of thing I'm thinking we could arrange for you – just for the rehearsal period for the concert. If you were living closer to school, you'd be able to fit everything in. What do you think?"

Bethany nodded slowly. It seemed like the perfect answer. "But … where would I live?" she asked a little anxiously.

"Well, the school has a sort of boardinghouse a couple of streets away. Some of the older students stay there," Miss Jasper explained.

"I should think they can fit you in for a

couple of weeks. It quite often gets used for that kind of thing. I'll talk to your form teacher about it and she can get in touch with your mum. OK?"

Bethany nodded, feeling a little dazed. The idea of not living at home was pretty scary, but at the moment most of her mind was full up with *I can do the concert after all!*

"Hey, Bethany!" Someone bounced up in front of Bethany as she walked slowly out of the office. "What were you talking to Miss Jasper about?" It was Chloe, looking even bubblier than usual. Excitement about the concert was practically oozing out of her.

"We were trying to work out how I can still do the concert—" Bethany started to explain, but Chloe interrupted, looking suddenly horrified.

"*Still* do it? What do you mean? Why shouldn't you be able to do it? What's happened?"

Bethany giggled at her panicked face – it was nice that somebody else really wanted her to be there! "Calm down! It's just that I realized on the bus this morning that it's going to be really hard to do after-school rehearsals, and get home afterward and fit in homework and everything."

Chloe looked doubtful. Homework was definitely not her top priority and she was a bit surprised that Bethany seemed so worried about it.

"I've already been in loads of trouble this week," Bethany explained. "I'm just scared they might take me out of the concert group if they think I can't cope." It was almost the truth...

Chloe nodded. *That* she could understand. "That would be awful," she murmured. "So, did Miss Jasper say anything that might help?"

"Yeah – she reckons I might be able to go and stay in a student house around the corner until the concert. She's going to get Miss James to call my mum. My sister'll be over the moon getting our bedroom all to herself."

Chloe looked amazed. "Wouldn't you mind being away from home?" she asked curiously. "I don't think I'd like it. When I did filming before, they always arranged for my mum to come too – I was only nine so I think they had to."

Bethany shrugged. "Well, it'll be a bit weird, I suppose. But it might be fun. Anyway, loads of people our age go to boarding school, don't they? It'll only be like that. I just hope my mum says I can."

The bell went then and they had to tear off to registration in a hurry. When they got there, Bethany shared her news with Lily and Sara.

Sara was almost jealous – although her mum was resigned to her being at Shine now, she still didn't really approve and she kept a watchful eye on Sara's homework. "She's always checking to make sure we're being taught to the same standard as at her school," Sara grumbled. "But I think we must be – she was looking at my science book last week and she looked really disappointed."

Sara grinned to herself. "I'll have to tell my gran about you going to stay there, Bethany. She was always staying in boardinghouses when she was a dancer. She said you never knew what they'd be like – some of them were lovely, but lots of them had horrible old ladies in charge who measured how much bathwater you used!"

Lily nodded. Her mum often had good show business stories. "Yeah, my mum said she stayed somewhere once and they had the same porridge reheated at breakfast time every day for a week. They all lived on sandwiches for that play and gave their food to the cat."

"It's very grown-up, staying on your own," Sara added. "Do you think your mum will be OK with it?"

"It's not really on my own," Bethany explained. "There's a sort of housemother who looks after everybody and Miss Jasper said she wouldn't be surprised if other people from the concert group had to stay too. No one from our year will though, will they? Jade and Daisy and Aiden don't have to travel that far. Where does Sam live?"

"Actually, I think he does have to do a horrible journey. He was moaning about his trains being late all last week," Chloe said thoughtfully.

"Hmm, I'm not sure I'd want to share a house with Sam," said Sara, wrinkling her nose. "You'd never know when you might find a spider in your bag or something."

Bethany nodded. "I know what you mean. But it would be nice to know somebody. I still don't know who the other four people in the group are. Did Mr. Harvey say they were Year Eights?"

Sara nodded. "I think so. It might be Amy and Izzy, who did the audition for *Mary Poppins* with me – they've got good voices. And they were really nice. If I see Nathan around today, I'll ask him." Nathan was playing Michael Banks, Sara's brother in *Mary Poppins*.

Chloe giggled. "What are the chances of you *not* seeing him? He pops up everywhere, Sara! I bet he's got the cafeteria staked out, waiting for you to arrive so he can accidentally on purpose come and sit with us."

Sara blushed. "That's not true," she protested, but she didn't sound very convinced. "I'm not sure what's going on with that," she admitted. "Sometimes I think he *might* be interested, but he probably just wants to talk about the show, that's all." She

went even redder as the other three crowed
with laughter.

"He's so going to ask you out," Bethany said
firmly. "He's probably just worried you'll say
no and then it'll be really difficult working
with you."

Chloe nodded wisely. "It's your duty to put
the poor thing out of his misery," she agreed.

Miss Jasper had obviously worked fast, as Miss
James seemed to be totally clued in on the
situation when she came to do the register. "I'll
give your mum a call at break, Bethany, and
see what she thinks," she said, making a note
to herself.

"Thanks, Miss James." Bethany shook her
head slightly. It was all happening so quickly!
How did she really feel about staying away
from home? She had hardly done it before,

except for a school trip in her last year at primary school and that was only a weekend. She supposed she would just have to see what it was like, but at the moment she felt more excited than nervous, which had to be a good sign.

Miss James popped into their form room at break to say that she'd spoken to Bethany's mum, who was fine about her staying in the school house. She would stay Monday, Tuesday, Wednesday and Thursday nights, and go home on Fridays. That would fit in with the rehearsals too, although there might be a couple the weekend before the concert that she'd have to come in specially for.

Bethany just nodded. Wow. It was a good thing she *wasn't* nervous about staying away. She was pretty sure her mum would miss her though. She wondered if Miss James had needed to persuade her at all – Serena and Bethany were very close to their mum, especially since it was only the three of them. Still, it was only for a couple of weeks and then she, Bethany Adams, was going to be on stage with Jasmine Day!

Sara clicked her fingers under Bethany's nose, laughing. "Snap out of it, Bethany! We've got to get to history. Were you planning wild midnight parties in your new house?"

Bethany shook her head. "No, just thinking about the concert." She looked at Sara thoughtfully. Would her friend understand if she explained a bit about how she'd been feeling? Chloe and Lily were off getting their books from their lockers, so it was a good chance to talk to Sara alone. "I'm really glad I'm going to be in it," she explained, and then realized that Sara was giving her a "Well, yeah!" kind of look. "I mean because all of the rest of you have done so well getting parts – I was feeling a bit useless."

"Oh! You muppet!" Sara gave her a hug. "I know what you mean, though. I'd have felt the same if it was me, but it's all just luck, isn't it? But you know you've got a brilliant voice. This concert's just going to be the start, I bet."

Sara's prediction didn't help Bethany's daydreaming. Or rather, it did – too much. Which was a bit dangerous, as Mr. Townsend hadn't been impressed with the class's history homework – Bethany's rushed piece had only gotten a C – and he was not in a patient mood. Bethany had to make a real effort to concentrate through their double period, and she was glad to get to lunch.

"Oooh, look who's here." Chloe sniggered into her orange juice. "There's a surprise, Sara!"

Nathan was strolling past, trying to look as

though he hadn't noticed them.

"Oh, but that's good!" Sara waved at him, and he hurried over eagerly. "We can ask him if he knows who else is in your backing group."

Nathan squashed himself in on the end of the table, as close to Sara as he could, despite Chloe cruelly telling him there was loads of space by her.

He nodded when Bethany asked about the concert. "Yeah, there are four people from our year. Amy – you remember her, Sara? And a friend of mine called Ethan, he's cool. And, er…" He trailed off, just as someone tapped Bethany on the shoulder. She'd been listening intently as she knew a few of the Year Eights by sight, and she was wondering if it would be someone who seemed nice, so she jumped at the unexpected touch.

Lizabeth, the stunning blond Year Eight girl who'd tried to trick Sara out of her *Mary*

Poppins audition, was standing behind her.

"… and Lizabeth and Nadia," Nathan
finished, shrugging apologetically.

"Guess what, Bethany?" Lizabeth cooed
sweetly. "Looks like you and I are sharing a
room for the next two weeks. It's going to be
such fun!"

CHAPTER FOUR
Living with the Enemy

It was a bombshell. The news that Lizabeth was also going to be staying in the school house almost (but not quite) destroyed Bethany's excitement about the concert. How *did* Lizabeth do it? Bethany supposed it was because she was so pretty and, admittedly, she did have a lovely singing voice with a crystal-clear tone to it.

"I didn't know she lived out of London," Lily said in horror.

Bethany was still too thunderstruck to say anything. She watched as Lizabeth triumphantly stalked out of the cafeteria, Nadia and the rest of her little gang trailing after her.

"We wouldn't, would we?" Sara muttered. "Oh, Bethany! I'm really sorry! Are you going to be OK with this?"

"Perhaps you could tell Miss James you'd rather stay at home after all?" Chloe suggested. "I mean, keeping up with your homework – it's not that vital, is it? Not if it means two weeks of living with Lizabeth."

Bethany gritted her teeth and then smiled – a slightly scary combination. It made her look like a fierce little lapdog. "It can't be that bad, can it? I mean, what can she *do*?"

The others were looking doubtful, especially Nathan, who had more experience dealing with Lizabeth, being in her year. "You'd be surprised," he muttered darkly.

But Bethany knew she didn't have a choice.
She was sure that she wouldn't be able to keep
her place in the concert group if her work
slipped any more. She would just have to cope
with Lizabeth…

When Bethany's mum got home, Bethany
didn't know what to say to her. She was pretty
sure that her mum would be worried about
the idea of her being away from home and she
didn't want to put her off the plan even more
– she couldn't bear to miss out on the concert.
But how could she be enthusiastic when it
meant sharing a room with Lizabeth? She'd
tried talking to Serena about it, but her sister
wasn't very helpful. Normally Bethany didn't
care what people said about her, so Serena
couldn't get her head around why Bethany was

so scared of Lizabeth. She thought it was just silly nerves. And she was *very* happy about getting their room to herself for a fortnight.

Bethany's mum seemed to be most worried about getting Bethany all packed over the weekend. Apparently it would be a total disaster if Bethany didn't go away with her entire wardrobe washed and ironed, and about six sets of spare everything. On Sunday, Bethany got the feeling she was lucky not to be sitting on the sofa wrapped in a towel while Mum shoved everything she owned into the machine. "I'm mostly only going to need my uniform, Mum!" she protested. "I'm only taking one extra bag, you know. Where do you think I'm putting all that?"

"You never know," her mother muttered, frantically folding.

Bethany got the feeling that her mum was worrying so much about the washing so that she didn't have to worry about everything else. She went over and gave her mum a hug. "It'll be OK, you know," she murmured in her ear.

Scarily, even though Bethany was tiny, she was almost as tall as her mum. It made her feel very grown up and very scared at the same time. It was so weird not to be able to spill out all her problems to her mum like she usually did – to know that she couldn't even mention Lizabeth and how mean she was. But she didn't want to make her worry anymore, so she just hugged her mum tighter instead.

Bethany's commute was even worse than
usual on Monday, as she was lugging the huge
extra bag to take to the school boardinghouse
with her. She hadn't managed to persuade her
mum that most of the washing was completely
unnecessary. Everyone else on the bus kept
giving her dirty looks as they bumped into
her stuff, and she felt like yelling, "It's not
my fault! Do you think I want to be dragging
this around with me?" It just showed that she
was feeling really nervous, not like herself at
all. And she still had to get through a day of
school before she even went to the house.

It was all made worse because she kept
passing Lizabeth in the corridors. The older
girl would flick her long blond hair at Bethany
and grin like a shark.

Luckily for Bethany, there was a lot going

on to distract her. Ms. Shaw sent for Chloe and Lily at morning break to give them their scripts for *Little Women*, and the whole class spent the rest of the day poring over them at every opportunity, while Lily and Chloe gazed blissfully at their lines. Lily kept stroking the cover of her script whenever someone else wasn't reading it.

"You're on all of this page and this one, wow, and this one as well." Chloe's friend Sam was leaning over her shoulder at the lunch table and flicking through the script. "Lots of learning, Chloe – your favorite thing."

Chloe grinned at him. "I know, but it's not like learning stuff for school, is it? Lines are different. Loads more interesting." She turned to Lily. "And we can practice together, Lily, which will be cool."

Lily bounced in her chair. Bethany thought she'd never seen her look so relaxed and happy. "I know. It's going to be brilliant. And anyway you can't talk, Mr. Four-out-of-twenty. And don't you dare drop ketchup on that script!"

Sam just grinned. Clearly he couldn't care less about bad marks in French. Bethany felt like kicking him.

Chloe tugged the script back from Sam. "Hey, let me see that bit. It's an outdoor scene. In the snow! Where are they going to find snow? That'll have to be on location, won't it?" She beamed. "Did we tell you some of the filming's going to be in the States?"

Everyone groaned and Sara kicked her.

"Only about half a million times."

Chloe grinned apologetically. "Sorry. I'll shut up now, I promise."

"Don't be silly!" Bethany couldn't help feeling a tiny bit guilty. Who wouldn't be excited? "You should be making a fuss, you deserve it." Then she put on an evil smirk. "Of course, if you keep going on about it, we might not let you live long enough to actually *get* to the filming…" She chuckled as Chloe gazed worriedly back at her, clearly trying to work out just how serious she was. "I don't mean it, Chloe! Everyone's happy for you. Really!"

"We didn't tell you the rest of our news," Lily said smugly. "Guess where we're going tonight."

"America!" Sam sniggered, and Lily and Chloe glared at him.

"You've got ketchup on your chin," Lily told him frostily, but Sam only shrugged.

"Where then?"

"A photo shoot!" Chloe's dark-blue eyes were sparkling. "The production company want to make a really big buzz about the series, Miss Shaw said, so they want publicity photos – even before we start filming!"

"That's a bit risky," Sam muttered worriedly, and the girls gave him confused looks. He'd managed a very convincing anxious voice. "Well, you know, they don't want to put everybody off, Chloe."

"OK, that's it." Chloe flounced up, grabbed Sam's tray and smacked it down on another table, next to a group of surprised and rather haughty Year Nines. "You're so not funny!"

"Aw, Chloe! Can't you take a joke anymore?" Sam moaned. "Now I've got to go and beg them for my lunch back! Hey! He's eating my pudding!" And he shot off to rescue his tray, leaving Chloe and the others giggling hysterically.

★ ★ ★

Miss James had told Bethany that she'd be walked over to the house at the end of school, and she swept Bethany downstairs with her. Sara, Lily and Chloe had all given her massive goodbye hugs, and Bethany was starting to feel like she'd been given a death sentence. Lizabeth was waiting by the school gates, with a set of cool pink bags that Bethany would have quite liked if they hadn't been Lizabeth's.

"Have you met Lizabeth, Bethany?" Miss James asked, smiling. She clearly had no idea about Bethany and Lizabeth's history. But then, why would she? Lizabeth's talent was for getting at people in ways that never got her noticed by teachers.

Lizabeth smiled charmingly at Miss James. "I've auditioned with Sara," she said, her voice sugar sweet. "So I've seen Bethany around."

Bethany bristled. Right, well, if Lizabeth was going to bring *that* up, it was clear that there was no truce going on here. Lizabeth was sending her a message that it was going to be a fight from the start.

They set off, Lizabeth chattering politely to Miss James and Bethany trying hard not to look like a sulky baby trailing after them.

The house was a tall, narrow one in a smart row a couple of streets away from the school. It had window boxes and nice curtains and looked quite friendly. As they climbed the front steps, a group of older students came out, all laughing and chatting, and Miss James explained that they would be from the one-year diploma course that Shine ran for over-sixteens. She led them into a tiny office in the hallway and a dark-haired lady on the phone waved apologetically at them. "Won't be long!" she mouthed, rolling her eyes.

Eventually she got rid of her caller and bounced up from behind her desk. "Lizabeth and Bethany, yes? I'm Ms. Robbins. I run the house. Let's take you up to your room. You're lucky, it's a very nice one."

Miss James checked her watch and said, "I need to go, girls, so I'll see you tomorrow. Have a nice evening!"

Bethany gazed after her. She might not actually *like* math, but Miss James was the last familiar thing she had being torn away from her. Except for Lizabeth, of course.

She was all *too* familiar.

Ms. Robbins went on chatting as they headed up the stairs, explaining how the house was really full at the moment and that they were lucky to be fit in. She led them into a room on the second floor and Bethany looked around delightedly. It was much bigger than the room she shared with Serena at home, and she gave a little gasp as Ms. Robbins showed them the tiny en suite bathroom in one corner. Total luxury!

Lizabeth glanced around haughtily, as if she was being forced to live in a pigsty. She dumped her bags on one of the beds and sneered at the bathroom.

Ms. Robbins handed each of them a printed sheet. "Sorry, girls, but these are the rules for younger students living in the house. We have to be quite strict – effectively we're taking the place of your parents for the next couple of weeks."

"My parents aren't strict at all," Lizabeth muttered, running down the list of rules disgustedly. "We have to be back in the house by *six o'clock*?"

"Well, unless you have something else arranged," Ms. Robbins replied calmly. "You two will be having rehearsals past then anyway, won't you?"

Bethany nodded. "The first one's tomorrow." And despite the awfulness of Lizabeth, she could feel little bubbles of excitement fizzing in her tummy. A rehearsal for her first professional engagement!

When Ms. Robbins went back downstairs, leaving them to "settle in," Bethany sat down on the bed Lizabeth hadn't claimed and wondered what to do next. They would have tea in half an hour or so and there was a common room with a TV, but she felt on edge. She hadn't quite gotten her head around sleeping in the same room with Lizabeth till now, when she saw how close together their beds were.

"So, do you share a room at home then?" Lizabeth was sitting cross-legged on her bed, clutching an old toy cat and gazing at Bethany in a weirdly hungry way.

"Yes," Bethany said cautiously. It was crazy, but she somehow felt that it was dangerous to give Lizabeth any information at all.

"Who with?"

"My sister," Bethany admitted reluctantly. "Why do you want to know?"

Lizabeth shrugged and smiled. "Just being

friendly. Seeing as we're going to be together so much."

Bethany shuddered slightly. Lizabeth being nice was scarier than Lizabeth in full demon mode. She thought back to when Lizabeth suddenly started being so sweet about Sara's *Mary Poppins* audition. And *then* look what happened, she thought to herself.

"So, you live way out, south of London then?" Lizabeth fished delicately. "What do your parents do?"

"My mum's a hairdresser," Bethany muttered. "My dad's not around anymore." She'd only been two when her dad had left and she didn't really remember him enough to mind, but sometimes other people were funny about it. But she was really proud of her mum, coping the way she had, and there was no way she was going to let Lizabeth think anything different.

"Wow! How does your mum manage to pay for you to be here? Sorry to be rude and everything, but I wouldn't have thought a hairdresser would earn enough for the fees at Shine." Lizabeth was leaning forward inquisitively, her deep-blue eyes fixed on Bethany's. It felt like she was sucking the information out of her.

"She's a very good hairdresser!" Bethany snapped, getting a little of her fierceness back.

"Mmmm," purred Lizabeth silkily. "Shine does scholarships. Did you know? Maybe you ought to have applied for one of those."

Bethany shifted on the bed. Lizabeth was getting a bit too close for comfort now. Her nose was actually twitching, as if she was a dog on a scent. She *knew* she had struck gold.

"Hey! That's it, isn't it?" she cooed. "You *do* have a scholarship! That's so cool, Bethany, I'm really impressed. You must have done so well at your audition." She was beaming now, but Bethany could feel how fake the smile was. *Yeah, right. Impressed by her own cleverness, more like.*

Bethany nibbled the side of her thumbnail, feeling panicky. Now that Lizabeth had this information, the big question was what was she going to do with it? She looked up at the Year Eight girl, wondering what would happen next.

Lizabeth bounced up from her bed. "We should go and get tea, don't you think? We can chat more later." And she actually linked arms with Bethany to lead her down the stairs. It felt like holding on to a dead fish.

By bedtime, Lizabeth had obviously worked out her plan. She was clever enough to have realized, from the way that Bethany hadn't wanted to admit to having a scholarship, that she hadn't told anyone about it. So now she was making the most out of this. Everything she said seemed to contain a sly little dig about money or charity or "But of course you wouldn't be able to afford that..." in a pitying kind of way.

But the worst thing she said came after they'd turned the lights out, and Bethany was lying there wondering if she'd ever be able to get to sleep with such a poisonous creature only six feet away from her.

"Of course, you managed ever so well picking your friends," Lizabeth said thoughtfully, and Bethany tensed up. Where was she going with this? "I mean, Lily's parents have got to be absolutely loaded and I'd guess Chloe's aren't hard up either. Not so sure about Sara. But getting to be best friends with a girl whose mum's on TV every other day was very clever. They don't know, of course?" She correctly interpreted Bethany's silence. "No, I thought not," she said triumphantly. "Pretty good for a scholarship girl." She yawned sleepily, and turned over. "Night night, Bethany."

CHAPTER FIVE
The Lizabeth Torture

Lizabeth brightened up breakfast the next day with a chatty series of comments about how *surprised* Lily and the others would be to find out about Bethany's scholarship. She wasn't saying *when* she was planning to tell them – that wasn't her style. She was going for long-drawn-out torture. And Bethany couldn't decide what to do about it. All her instincts were screaming, "Tell Lily and the others yourself now, before that blond witch does it for you!" But Lizabeth had been very clever.

Even in the short time she'd had, she'd managed to make Bethany feel as though she'd done something very sly by not telling everyone about her scholarship, and then making friends with Lily, whose parents were really well off – as if the whole thing had been some cunning plan.

It wasn't true, of course. Bethany hadn't even known who Lily's mum was when she found Lily in a tearful heap on their first day – after Lizabeth herself had been so cruel to her. But Lizabeth was scarily good at setting people up, and Bethany was almost starting to feel like she *had* done it on purpose. And if *she* felt like that, what would the others think? Bethany couldn't bear the idea that her friends might think she'd been playing some horrible game the whole time – she just didn't know what to do.

She was plucking up the courage to talk to them about it as she and Lizabeth walked into school. Lizabeth said goodbye to her almost affectionately and headed off to the Year Eight form room, leaving Bethany practically grinding her teeth with frustration as she climbed the stairs. How could *anyone* be so fake?

Sara jumped on her as soon as she walked in the door. "Are you OK? What was it like? Was she horrible to you? And why didn't you text me?"

Bethany grinned, some of the tension that had been gripping her since yesterday afternoon easing away. Sara *was* a real friend. She'd been wrong to doubt it. "Ish, scary, yes, and sorry, I was going to, but I couldn't get away from the slime lizard. That's my new name for her, by the way."

"Suits her." Sara was grinning in relief. "I'm so glad to see you. I thought you'd be a total wreck."

"I almost am." Bethany took a deep breath. "Look, I ought to tell you—"

"There they are!" A delighted screech was followed by Chloe and Lily racing up to them at top speed.

"Hey, what's happened?" Sara grabbed Chloe's arms to hold her in one place – their redheaded friend seemed to have turned into a meerkat suddenly and couldn't stop twisting around.

"Look!" Lily waved a scrap of paper under their noses.

"Hold still, we can't read it," Bethany complained. "What is it?"

Lily handed it to her, beaming. "It's a newspaper article. From Chloe's mum's paper this morning."

As Bethany and Sara bent over the newspaper, Chloe started dancing around the classroom. Then she grabbed Lily and made her waltz up and down too.

"It's all about the series. Hey, that's amazing!" Bethany forgot about Lizabeth immediately.

"And have you read the best bit?" Chloe squawked. "Skip to the end! Oh, go on, the bit in the middle's just boring stuff about the director, read the end!"

"What? Ummm, shot partly in Britain, partly in America, we knew that. Lavish production… Wow, that's a lot of money… Ashton Smith's going to be in it! No! Sara, look! Really?" Bethany scanned the short paragraph again.

"Only maybe," Lily cautioned. "He's not signed up for definite yet."

"Don't be so sensible, Lily. It's really boring!" Chloe hauled her on another waltz around the room. "We're going to America WITH THE WORLD'S CUTEST ACTOR EVER!"

Lily's phone beeped and she laughed as she read the message. "My mum's seen it too. She says now we just have to win a couple of BAFTAs. She's really pleased." Lily's face was glowing.

Something jolted in Bethany's stomach. Lily's mum. Lily's rich, successful actress mum.

Lizabeth. In the excitement of the news she'd actually forgotten about Lizabeth's torture for a second. Now was clearly not the time to have a heart-to-heart with any of her friends. She felt so angry with Lizabeth for spoiling this moment. She ought to be laughing with Lily and Chloe, begging for more exciting details and finding out about the photo shoot, but Lizabeth's veiled threats were at the back of her mind the whole time.

It was the same all day. Everyone seemed to have seen the article, and Lily and Chloe were like school celebrities. People kept pointing them out as they passed them in the corridors. Mr. Lessing, their acting teacher, stopped the girls on their way to ballet to congratulate them. He'd been brilliant about coaching Lily and Chloe for the auditions, so they spent ages telling him about the photo shoot. It turned out that he knew half the actors who were

going to be in the series and he promised to
tell them some juicy gossip in their next drama
class.

Their excited conversation with each
other left Bethany free to notice Lizabeth
pattering past on her way to a tap class,
smiling secretively and giving her a tiny wave.
Bethany felt sick.

Even the rehearsal for the concert wasn't
as special as it
should have
been. Well, it
was special,
and Bethany
almost
managed to
forget what
was going
on, but
Lizabeth

was there too, and however much Bethany tried to stay with Chloe and avoid her, she couldn't shut her out of her mind completely.

But singing Jasmine Day's lyrics was amazing. Rehearsing how to sing the backing tracks to some of her favorite songs properly and learning all the cool harmonies was so different than just singing along with the radio.

The rehearsal was in a hired studio, which a lot of the artists for the concert were also using. Jasmine herself wasn't there, of course – she wouldn't be until the last couple of rehearsals – but Bethany was certain she recognized a few of the dancers from Jasmine's music videos. She and Chloe kept whispering together about it in the breaks and Sam thought it was really funny. Unsurprisingly, he wasn't a big Jasmine Day fan and so he wasn't quite as starstruck. "Why don't you just ask if they've been on TV backing her?" he said, grinning, and they shushed him in horror.

"I can't wait till we're actually rehearsing at the Albert Hall next week," Chloe said dreamily, as they walked out. "It's such a brilliant venue – so grand."

Bethany nodded. "I'm so excited – I've never even been there," she admitted.

"Well, it's a bit of a long way for you, isn't it, Bethany?" Lizabeth cooed from behind her. "Bit of a step up." And she sailed past, following the school chaperone who was fussing about the arrangements to get them all home.

"What's she talking about?" Sam asked Bethany.

"No idea," Bethany answered, trying not to let her voice tremble. "She gets weirder every day, I think."

Sam nodded and seemed to be satisfied, but

Chloe was gazing after Lizabeth suspiciously. Bethany changed the subject quickly. "So how come you're not having to stay up here?" she asked Sam. "Chloe said you had a nightmare journey too."

"They did think about it." Sam nodded. "But certain people – " here he rolled his eyes at Bethany – "had already bagged the last room at the house, and we worked out that if my older brother stays a bit late at work he can pick me up halfway. It's all a bit complicated though and he reckons I really owe him. I'm going to be washing his motorbike every weekend for the rest of my life."

Bethany had escaped that one catty comment from Lizabeth, but she knew it was only the beginning. And she was right. Lizabeth was getting worse and worse, niggling at her when they were together and making nasty comments about how Lily, Chloe and Sara would hate Bethany when they found out what she'd done, and they'd tell everyone else what a liar she was. Bethany was sure it wasn't true or at least, she had been…

Lizabeth made cryptic remarks in front of Bethany's friends whenever she saw them at school, too. Luckily, no one else seemed to pick up on these. Chloe and Lily were so caught up in the excitement about *Little Women* that you'd practically have to sledgehammer them over the head with a hint before they got it. And Sara was up to her neck in rehearsals for *Mary Poppins* and trying to work out what was really going on with her and Nathan.

Bethany was really glad that her secret was still safe – it was exactly what she'd been hoping for. But none of her friends seemed to notice how upset she was, or that she was getting quieter and quieter at school. She was beginning to worry that maybe Lizabeth was right, and it was obvious that the others had more important things to think about than her. And if they didn't really care about her, then they *would* think that she'd lied to them on purpose, and then they'd all hate her. Bethany was so confused.

She had the added problem that staying at the school house wasn't helping her schoolwork much either. Lizabeth was making her so miserable she couldn't concentrate, and she'd been told off in class a couple of times since moving in.

But on Friday morning, Bethany woke up feeling happy. She was going home tonight! Even Lizabeth's mean comments at breakfast didn't seem as bad as before and Bethany felt a bit more optimistic. She shouldn't be letting Lizabeth get to her like this. *I'll talk to the others about it today,* she promised herself, and she actually managed a "don't care" grin at Lizabeth's latest little "joke."

At break she found her opportunity. She thought it would be easier to talk to just one of her friends to start with, especially as she didn't know what she was going to say yet. Chloe and Lily had gone off to the cafeteria to get snacks, leaving Sara and Bethany in their classroom, flicking through a magazine. No one else was close by and Bethany realized this was it. She took a deep breath.

"Sara?"

"Mmmm? Do you think her hair looks good like that?" Sara twisted her head around to look at the picture a different way. "Nope. Still looks terrible. She should never have cut it off, I don't think." She shook her own long blond hair happily.

"Sara!" Bethany's voice was a little irritable now. When you were trying to bare your soul, it was very annoying if people didn't listen. "I need to talk to you about something."

"What?" Sara looked up interestedly. "Oh, did you find out more about the concert? Did they tell you what you're going to wear yet?"

"Um, yes, they said it would be white." Bethany was temporarily distracted from her mission. "White and silver. It should look good, I think."

"It's so unfair you get to wear a cool white

outfit and I'm stuck in a pinafore dress for *Mary Poppins*. I saw the design – it's covered in bows. Seriously!"

Bethany frowned. It obviously wasn't going to be easy to get Sara to listen. She tried again. "Anyway—"

Just then Nathan popped his head around the classroom door. Sara seemed to brighten when she saw him and she sat up straighter, her eyes beginning to sparkle. Bethany slumped next to her. What was the point? Sara wasn't interested. *Maybe nobody is*, she thought pathetically. Then she sighed sadly as she watched Sara blushing and talking eagerly with Nathan about something. *Grow up, Bethany*, she told herself. *It was a silly idea anyway.* She sighed. She'd just have to cope with whatever Lizabeth was going to dig up on her own. Roll on the weekend…

Bethany felt awful going back to school on Monday – much worse after her weekend's break from the Lizabeth torture. In between being miserable, she just felt furious, partly with Lizabeth but mostly with herself. How could she be letting someone upset her so much?

Knowing it was silly didn't help, though. Bethany was feeling like a nervous wreck, ready to quiver into a pool of jelly the next time Lizabeth so much as looked at her. Even the thought of their first rehearsal with

Jasmine Day that Tuesday evening couldn't really cheer her up.

Still, it was amazing to see the star march into the studio, accompanied by her huge entourage. Bethany couldn't help dreaming that that would be her one day. She felt Chloe squeeze her hand in excitement. They were about six feet away from Jasmine Day!

Jasmine turned out to be really nice. She insisted on being told all of their names and she even admired the purple dip dye that Bethany's mum had done for her. Bethany glowed, until she caught a glimpse of Lizabeth looking furious – she was the one whose looks usually got admired. She glared dangerously at Bethany, who felt her throat go dry.

In the last rehearsal, she, Lizabeth and Amy had been given a complicated harmony to sing together in one of the songs. Bethany

loved it – it was one of those pieces of music that just sounded so right. But now she couldn't even remember the notes. When they got to that song, "Flight," the last one they were rehearsing, all she could see was Lizabeth, holding her gaze like a snake, hypnotizing her. She tried to sing out as she'd been taught, but her voice seemed to be stuck in her throat. The voice coach for the group frowned at her and Bethany desperately tried again. But the notes were totally wrong and the song ground to a halt, with everybody staring at her.

The voice coach, Matt, apologized to Jasmine. "No idea what went wrong there," he said, staring grimly at Bethany as though he knew *exactly* what had gone wrong.

Bethany gulped, and suddenly she knew that she just couldn't do this. Not with Lizabeth right next to her, psyching her out.

There was no way.

"Perhaps we need to take a break?" a sweet voice suggested. It was Jasmine and she was smiling sympathetically at Bethany. "I know I could do with ten minutes."

Matt nodded. "OK. Back here in ten."

Bethany didn't know whether to laugh or cry. Jasmine Day had noticed her, but only because she'd totally messed up one of her most beautiful songs.

CHAPTER SIX
Chloe to the Rescue

Chloe grabbed Bethany and shoved her out of the studio at lightning speed before Matt could speak to her. "What on earth's the matter?" she demanded as soon as they got out of the door. "You could sing that perfectly last time. Is it just nerves because Jasmine's here?" She shook her head. "No, that's not like you. Come on, tell me!"

She hustled Bethany to a sofa by the drink machine and stared at her in the same information-sucking way that Lizabeth had. Somehow Chloe's stare was so different, though.

"Hey." A soft voice sounded behind them and both girls jumped. It was Jasmine, for once unaccompanied by her string of minders. Chloe looked around disbelievingly.

"Yeah, I managed to lose them." Jasmine sounded amused. "Chloe and Bethany, right?"

They nodded silently, awestruck. Not only was she talking to them, but she knew their names!

"So what happened? You've got a gorgeous voice, Bethany. I could hear you in the other songs. Then that harmony came along and you totally lost it. No way that was natural."

Bethany took a deep breath. What should she say? It would sound so lame to admit that Lizabeth had been freaking her out.

The singer crouched down by Bethany.

"It seemed to me like that tall, blond ice queen had something to do with it. That wasn't a friendly look she was giving you."

Bethany nodded, relieved that she didn't have to be the one to say it.

"Lizabeth?" Chloe asked sharply. "Bethany, why didn't you say? What's she been doing?"

Bethany shrugged. "Oh, she's just being Lizabeth, I guess."

"Don't let her get to you." Jasmine stood up, smiling. "Easy to say, I know. That's why I'm doing this concert, did you know that? Wish helps a lot of kids who've been bullied and I had the worst time at school – before I went to Shine. Tell someone next time, Bethany. Don't let her win. See you back there in a couple of minutes – you'll be fine singing it this time, I know you will."

She was right. No one who had just been told by a BRIT award-winning singer that she had a gorgeous voice could be put off using it, even with Lizabeth still around. But Lizabeth had the look of someone who thought she might have been outsmarted and wasn't quite sure how. She could obviously feel Bethany's new confidence.

"I'm amazed they're still letting you sing after that little performance," she sneered, and she looked positively furious when

Bethany just smiled at her.

"Leave her alone!" Chloe's voice was a scary kind of whispered snarl to avoid the others hearing. Lizabeth had to content herself with a meaningful look at Bethany. But even that couldn't put her off now.

Jasmine's praise had made the whole scholarship thing seem less important, and Chloe standing up for her made Bethany think that maybe she'd been wrong to doubt her friends. If she'd just found out she had a part in a West End musical, or she was going to film a drama series in America, *she* might not be totally on the ball with everybody else's problems either. The harmony soared above the tune and it seemed to Bethany that she could almost feel her voice intertwining with Jasmine's. The singer gave her a thumbs-up and a big smile, and Matt, the voice coach, looked delighted at the end of the song.

"A ten-minute break certainly helped *you*,"
he said, smiling at Bethany. "Like that on the
night please, everyone. Well, I think we're
nearly done – Jasmine, anything else you
want to run through today? Obviously we've
got another rehearsal at the Albert Hall on
Thursday afternoon and sound checks before
the concert on Friday night."

Jasmine shook her head, smiling. "No, it
was all sounding great. Oh, one thing actually.
I just wonder if that new song could do with
something a little more? You know what I mean?

I think it's got room for another voice, to give it a bit more depth. I'd like to talk to Chas about putting in a solo for Bethany on it." She grinned at Bethany. "You'd be all right with that, wouldn't you? You'd have time to learn it? Mr. Harvey's still at Shine isn't he? He'll just *love* teaching you a pop solo."

Bethany giggled at the thought of Mr. Harvey's face. "I'd love it," she said quietly.

"That's it then. See you on Thursday, everybody." And she swept out, leaving the backing group to gather around Bethany in amazement.

Everyone got whisked off home after the rehearsal, and Bethany realized with a sudden jolt that this meant she was back at the mercy of Lizabeth, who was not a happy bunny. She simmered with rage the whole way back to the house, and as soon as they were alone in their bedroom she exploded.

"Just you wait, Bethany! You wait until I tell everybody what you did—"

"I didn't do anything!" Bethany protested. Jasmine and Chloe together had given her such a boost that she was starting to see Lizabeth's threats for what they really were. She still didn't want anyone to know about the scholarship – or at least, not until she'd found exactly the right moment to tell them – but she was feeling a bit more confident about her friends. "Maybe Nadia and all your little friends would drop you if you didn't have any money, but Lily and Chloe and Sara aren't like that." *Or I don't think they are, anyway*, she added to herself. "So just shut up and leave me alone, I'm going to sleep." And she pulled her pillow over her head to shut out any more of Lizabeth's taunts.

The next morning there was a stern reception committee waiting in the Year Seven form room. Chloe had updated Lily and Sara on what had happened at the rehearsal and they were looking fierce.

"Why didn't you tell us?" Lily burst out as soon as Bethany walked in the door. "We could have helped."

Sara was looking guilty. "Bethany, were you trying to talk to me at break on Friday? I can't believe I let Nathan stop you telling me!"

Bethany squirmed. She still didn't want to be anybody's sympathy case and Lizabeth's "charity girl" comments had really gotten to her. She could just imagine their faces all changing when they found out. OK, she was pretty sure they wouldn't stop being her friends, but they might *feel* differently about her. Sorry for her… No! She wouldn't let that happen! Even though Lizabeth still knew the truth, hopefully what Bethany had said to her last night would have convinced her that Bethany was going to tell her friends about the scholarship herself, which meant Lizabeth wouldn't tell them first.

"I didn't mean to not tell you. It was just – you all had so much going on. I didn't want to spoil things. I mean, you two were so happy, and Sara – it didn't seem fair…" She trailed off, and then added, "It was just Lizabeth being Lizabeth again, after all."

"Yes, and we know what that's like!" Lily cried. "She's a monster. You have to tell someone, Bethany."

Bethany sighed. "We didn't tell anyone when she was going after you or Sara. I'm not a baby, Lily. I can cope."

"That's crazy. It's not about you, it's about her!" Sara put in. "But I guess we can't make you. I should have told everybody what she did about the audition, but I was feeling so embarrassed that she'd managed to trick me."

"Exactly." Bethany nodded. "I know it's silly, but I don't want to give her the satisfaction."

"The satisfaction of being suspended?" Lily demanded crossly.

"There's no point us having a row about it too," Chloe said firmly. "Anyway, Bethany, hopefully it's not going to be a problem for much longer. We've got a plan. I know it's only another two nights, but you're not going back to that place with Lizabeth."

Bethany frowned, her nose wrinkling. "I suppose I could go back home. But then I'd have to explain why."

"Our plan is much better than that." Chloe grinned smugly. She looked so pleased with herself that Bethany was sure this was her idea. "Come and stay with me for the next two nights. *Pleeeease*, Bethany! I'd love it anyway, and it gets you away from Lizabeth and you'll be loads closer to school than if you went back home. My mum's got to get me from rehearsal anyway, so it's no extra bother for her. I'll even promise to do all my homework like an angel so I'm not distracting you!"

Bethany could feel tears pressing at the corners of her eyes. She couldn't believe that Chloe had arranged this. "Don't your parents mind?" she asked quaveringly.

"They think it's a great idea. My mum said please come, she'd love to meet you. I've told her about Lizabeth and she says there's no way you're going back there. She's going to call the school and sort it out, and your mum, as soon as I text her to say you're OK with it. So are you?"

Bethany nodded. "Yes, please. Oh, yes!" And she gave Chloe a grateful hug, still trying to blink away her tears.

Chloe hugged her back excitedly. "I can't

wait. I used to have people from school around all the time, but it's harder when we all live so far away from each other. It'll be like a fab two-night sleepover!" She grabbed her phone out of her bag. "I'll get Mum on to it right now."

School felt so different that day, as though a cloud had lifted. Even when Bethany saw Lizabeth in the corridors, the blond girl's scowling face had no effect – Bethany could beam back at her without caring. She loved the thought of Lizabeth not knowing where she was at the end of the day, probably wondering if Bethany had told someone about her bullying and how she'd had to go home. Bethany hoped Lizabeth would be sweating about it all night – while she was staying with Chloe!

At the end of school Chloe was like an anxious sheepdog, herding Bethany around to grab all her stuff. Bethany had been given special permission to go out at lunchtime to fetch her things from the school house, and now she had Chloe to help her carry them too. She'd had to explain to Miss James that she "really didn't get along" with Lizabeth, and that was why she was so desperate to go home with Chloe. But she managed not to make it sound too feeble.

"This is so cool," Chloe bubbled, as they crammed themselves onto her train. The journey was a bit hectic, but it only took half an hour. It seemed no time to Bethany before they were walking up the path of a huge-looking house. Bethany blinked. Chloe lived *here*? The front door opened and Chloe's mum pattered out looking delighted. She was really like Chloe, with the same red hair and chatty friendliness.

"Bethany! I'm so glad you've come to us. Chloe's told me about that awful girl. It sounds to me as though the school really needs to deal with her, and soon."

She hustled them inside and sent them to take all Bethany's stuff upstairs while she got some snacks ready. "We'll have a little something now and then dinner when Chloe's dad gets home later. You two can use the time to do your homework together, rather than Chloe doing it in front of her TV when she's supposed to be in bed." She gave Chloe a fake scowl and Chloe grinned innocently back. It was lovely – Bethany really felt that Chloe's mum was as pleased as Chloe to have her there.

Chloe's room was a bit of a shock. Bethany remembered her saying something before about her mum and dad letting her use some of the money from her ad work to buy herself a new computer – but it looked like Chloe had everything! For a start her room was enormous, with a huge bed, big closets all down one side – with clothes spilling out of them all over the place – and a whole media unit with every gadget imaginable.

"There's a sleepover bed under here," Chloe was explaining in a muffled voice as she rooted around under her bed. "Just have to find the right handle. There!" And she pulled a second bed out. "Mum's put sheets and everything out for us. Do you *really* want to do your homework? I thought we could watch a film or something."

Bethany considered. It did seem a waste. She fancied curling up on that comfy-looking bed – Chloe had loads of huge fluffy cushions scattered all over it – and watching a film.

"I've got popcorn," Chloe added, waving the bag temptingly. "Borrowed it out of the kitchen cupboard when Mum wasn't looking."

"We could do that science thing while we're watching a film maybe," Bethany said hopefully.

"Good plan. And then it's just learning that stuff for geography. We could test each other on that tomorrow when we get up, no problem. Excellent. Come on – Mum'll have gotten food ready for us. Do you want to change? I hate wearing my uniform at home." Chloe flung open one of her closet doors and grabbed jeans and a glittery T-shirt, and Bethany blinked at the number of clothes she had. And the shoes! *How* many pairs of shoes?

There was no question that it was going to be huge fun staying with Chloe, but as Bethany rootled through her bag for her sweatpants, she suddenly felt out of place. She so didn't want Chloe, the owner of all this stuff – who apparently had no idea how lucky she was, judging by the way she was complaining about never being able to shut her closet doors – to know what her little shared bedroom was like.

It wasn't that Bethany really thought Chloe wouldn't want to be friends with her any more. That had just been Lizabeth being evil. The effort Chloe had made to help Bethany showed her that she was a real friend. But she wasn't sure that Chloe would be able to get her head around the whole scholarship thing. And Bethany didn't fancy explaining it.

No. Her secret was just going to have to stay a secret for the time being.

CHAPTER SEVEN
The Truth Comes Out

"Hang on girls, I need to spray your hair!" A panicked-looking makeup artist was dashing around trying to make sure everyone was ready – the finishing touch was glitter hair spray to show up under the auditorium lights. She'd already managed to spray Sam and Aiden, who were scowling disgustedly at their sparkly hair in the big mirrors.

"I think you should wear that to school, Sam," Chloe giggled. "And baggy white trousers really suit you, Aiden. Definitely a cool new look for you."

"If anybody had mentioned white trousers and glitter before all this started, I'd have said no faster than the speed of light," Sam muttered.

"Yeah, right, as if you were going to say no to Mr. Harvey," Aiden mocked.

"Didn't you ever have to dress up for dance shows or anything like that?" Bethany asked the boys. She'd worn more silly costumes than she could count.

Sam grinned. "I usually managed to convince them that I wouldn't look good as a daisy or whatever it was. I was more the evil flower-eating snail type. Aaaargh! Delicious petalsssss!" He loomed over Bethany in an evil snail pose, and she and Chloe cracked up.

"Glittery evil snail!" Bethany spluttered. "I love it, Sam!"

The makeup artist scurried up to the girls. "I haven't done you two, have I? Oh, this is going to look lovely on your hair," she said to Bethany. She started playing with Bethany's dip-dyed hair and spraying it thoroughly.

Bethany couldn't help gazing into the mirror. They had a couple of very simple dance moves to do during their songs and she could tell that the glitter was going to be fabulous when she twirled around. She was pleased to find that she wasn't nervous at all. It was silly that someone like Lizabeth had gotten her into such a state over the last week, but performing at the Albert Hall just made her feel excited now.

"Are *you* nervous?" she asked Chloe curiously.

Chloe looked herself over, as though she expected to see a little sign saying yes or no. "No, I don't think so! I think I would be if I had your solo, but I'm really jealous too."

Bethany grinned. "It's great though – at the moment I don't even feel nervous about that. I'm just really looking forward to it. And I'm so glad my mum and Serena are here."

"Yeah, and Lily and Sara. It was nice of the concert people to give the school those tickets. I bet my mum can't even sit still out there right now! Ow!"

"Well, don't jump around when I'm brushing your hair," snapped the makeup girl, and Chloe rolled her eyes. "You've only got a couple of minutes before you need to go into the wings, so I need to get you done."

A runner with a headset appeared at the door. "Everyone ready?" he asked. "I need to take you up." The makeup girl released Chloe and everyone exchanged excited looks; even Lizabeth grinned at Nadia and Amy.

Lizabeth looked amazing, Bethany had to admit – like an ice maiden in her white trousers and vest top, with all that glittery blond hair flying. Bethany wondered, not for the first time, if she was such good friends with Nadia because Nadia wasn't nearly as pretty as she was. *That's really mean of you, Bethany Adams*, she told herself. *But probably true!* she added, smiling to herself.

It was amazing, standing in the wings and

watching everyone scurry around like crazy bees. "That's so-and-so, isn't it?" Chloe kept muttering in her ear, and it almost always was!

Bethany's solo part came in the last song they were singing, one that had been specially written for the concert. She had to stand with Jasmine at the front of the stage. As the previous song finished, she walked slowly up to the front, telling herself firmly not to go too fast – that was the hardest thing. Bethany wasn't worried about singing the song, but she was convinced she was going to fall on her face in front of five thousand people.

Jasmine beamed at her as the first notes of the song sounded, and Bethany grinned back happily. This was what she wanted to be doing for the rest of her life! Silly stuff like Lizabeth faded into the background as Jasmine put an arm around her waist and they started to sing, the others humming and swaying gently in the background.

Was it Bethany's imagination or could she hear Lily and Sara and Serena screaming her name out there?

At the end of the song, she scampered off the stage with the others, hardly able to believe it was over already. They crammed back into the dressing room and drank lemonade, all still on an adrenaline high. There was only one act after Jasmine, so it seemed just minutes later that Lily and Sara were flinging themselves into the room, followed by Chloe's parents, Bethany's mum and Serena.

"They let us come backstage," Lily said excitedly. "You were all brilliant. Well done! I think everyone's parents are fighting their way through security to come and see you all."

"I'm going to see if I can find my dad," Sam said, and a few of the others followed him.

"Bethany, your solo was amazing!" Sara hugged her. "I was so proud. I felt like nudging the people next to me and saying, 'I know her! She sits next to me in math!'"

Bethany's mum actually had tears in her eyes as she hugged her too. "It was so special, Bethany, I was really proud of you. We really did make the right decision letting you apply for that scholarship. I can't believe you've done so well."

Bethany felt all the color and excitement draining out of her face. After all her stress about hiding the scholarship, she hadn't even *thought* to warn her mum and Serena that she hadn't told anyone. Well, how could she? *It would be like saying that I think we're not good enough for Shine*, she thought to herself angrily. *I've been so wrong. I should have told everyone ages ago.*

She looked around at Chloe, Lily and Sara. As she'd expected, their faces were shocked. She braced herself – she had no idea what they were going to say.

"Bethany!" yelped Sara. "You never told us you had a scholarship!" Her eyes had darkened with surprise and gone huge and round.

Bethany's mum looked suddenly worried and gazed at her daughter anxiously. Bethany gripped her hand and tried to smile.

"That's so amazing," breathed Lily. "Do you *know* how many people were after that scholarship? Why didn't you say?"

"Still, after this evening I guess we shouldn't be surprised. When's your first album coming out, Bethany?" Chloe giggled. "You were even better than Jasmine."

Bethany's lungs stopped feeling as though they'd broken and she took in a deep breath. "I just never found a good moment to tell you. Um, sorry…"

Sara shook her head. "Why are you apologizing, silly? It's not one of those things you go around telling everybody, is it? 'Hi, I'm Bethany and I'm so outstandingly brilliant that Shine gave me a scholarship.'"

"We'd all have kicked you," Chloe said, smiling. "Actually, can I kick you now? Just to make sure you don't get too full of yourself."

Serena, who'd been perching next to Bethany against the dressing table, suddenly gulped and nodded toward the door. "Look," she whispered excitedly.

It was Jasmine, looking amazing in her stage costume, her face flushed with the excitement of the performance.

"Oh wow," Serena muttered, starstruck.

Jasmine smiled at everyone and then homed in on Bethany. "I just wanted to come and say well done." She grinned. "And also ask if you're busy early next year, because I'm recording the new album and I really like your voice. I'd like you to sing with me on a couple of tracks."

Bethany could feel Serena trembling with excitement next to her.

"Yes!" Bethany squeaked, her voice disappearing entirely. Over Jasmine's shoulder she caught sight of Lizabeth, frozen to the spot with horror. The scary, worried feeling that had been lurking inside her for the last couple of weeks suddenly disappeared, and she beamed at Jasmine. "Oh, yes, please!"

HOLLY WEBB

Holly Webb started out as a children's book
editor and wrote her first series for the
publisher she worked for. She has been writing
ever since, with over one hundred books to her
name. Holly lives in Berkshire, UK, with her
husband and three young sons. Holly's pet cats
are always nosying around when she is trying
to type on her laptop.

For more information
about Holly Webb visit:

www.holly-webb.com